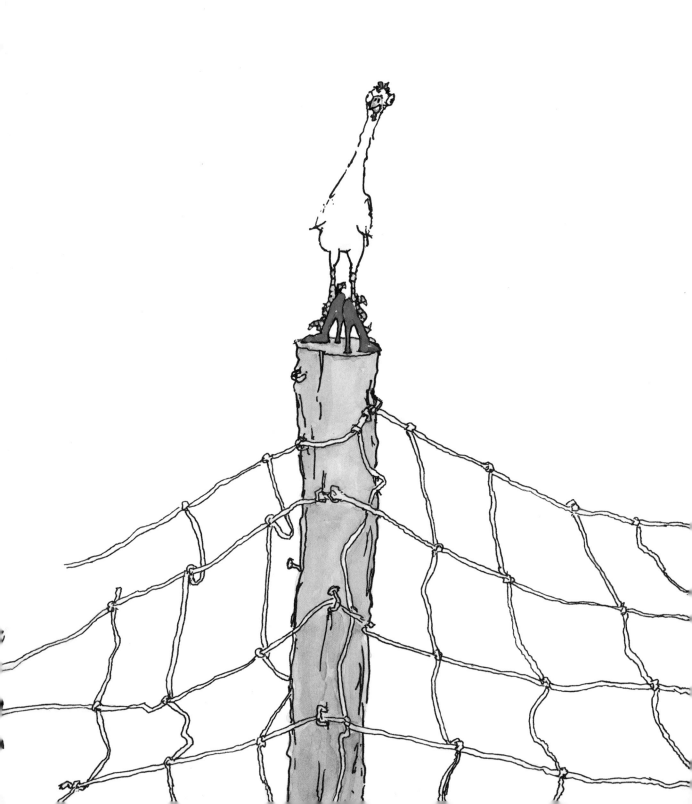

Harry Allard

STARLIGHT GOES TO TOWN

Pictures by
George Booth

Farrar, Straus and Giroux ❧ New York

For Claudio Galván and Coley C. Mills
—H.A.

For Master Sergeant John DeGrasse, U.S.M.C.
—G.B.

Text copyright © 2008 by Harry Allard
Pictures copyright © 2008 by George Booth
All rights reserved
Distributed in Canada by Douglas & McIntyre Ltd.
Color separations by Embassy Graphics
Printed and bound in the United States of America by Worzalla
Designed by Irene Metaxatos
First edition, 2008
1 3 5 7 9 10 8 6 4 2

www.fsgkidsbooks.com

Library of Congress Cataloging-in-Publication Data
Allard, Harry.
    Starlight goes to town / Harry Allard ; pictures by George Booth.— 1st ed.
        p. cm.
    Summary: Starlight LaPoule, better known as Ethel-Fae Klucksworth, is very unhappy
living on a poultry farm in Tennessee, but when her fairy godmother gives her the ability
to make her wishes come true, the results are unexpected.
    ISBN-13: 978-0-374-37187-6
    ISBN-10: 0-374-37187-3
    [1. Chickens—Fiction. 2. Fairy godmothers—Fiction. 3. Contentment—Fiction.
4. Humorous stories.] I. Title.

PZ7.A413 Snn 2008
[E]—dc22

                                                                            2006040852

Starlight LaPoule—(hush! Her real name
was Ethel Fae Klucksworth)—was unhappy.
"I do not belong on a poultry farm in
southeastern Tennessee," she said to anyone
who would listen.

Starlight dreamed of becoming a high-fashion model in New York, in London, in Paris, or in Milan (which, she had learned, is a city located in northern Italy).

All the other hens in Farmer Brown's henhouse thought Starlight was short a few feathers. Whenever she spoke of her dreams, they would jab one another in the ribs, and gleek and fleer at her. "Get a load of Ethel Fae!" they snickered.

But one night, Starlight was awakened by
someone who didn't laugh at her dreams.

"Allow me to introduce myself," the visitor said.
"My name is Melody D. Youngstown. I am your
fairy godmother."

She gave Starlight her card.

Melody D. Youngstown

Professional Chicken Fairy Godmother

United Chicken Fairy Godmothers of America, Inc.

A Non-Profit Organization

Home office: Akron, Ohio

Without beating around the bush, Starlight said,
"I want out of this dump."
"Who wouldn't, dear?" said Melody.
"What can I do?" asked Starlight.

"When you are ready to lay your next egg, just make a wish and utter my name. Then close your eyes tight, and whatever you wish will come true."

With that, Starlight's lovely fairy godmother vanished.

The very next morning, Starlight laid an egg.
It was gigantic.
All the other hens in Farmer Brown's henhouse
were sick with envy.

The egg cracked open.

Inside was a big, shiny, brand-new convertible.

Starlight jumped behind the steering wheel, switched on the ignition, floorboarded the gas, and sped off in a cloud of dust.

"So long, girls!" she shouted. "If I never see you again, it will be too soon."

When she got to the Atlantic Ocean, she wished for an airplane, laid an even larger egg, and took off for Italy in a two-seater.

After navigating the peaks of the Dolomite mountains, Starlight landed in Milan, where she lost no time in appearing in a fashion show as a top model.

Everyone laughed when Starlight sashayed down the catwalk.

"Sheesh!" sniffed Starlight. "These people are too dumb to recognize a truly great and beautiful chicken model when they see one."

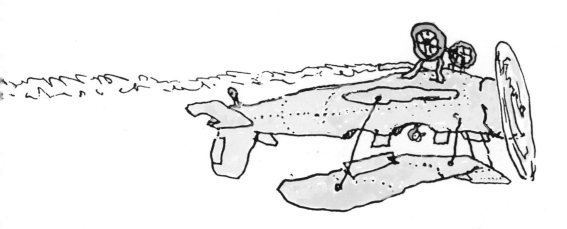

Starlight decided to return to the United States,
but not to the henhouse in southeastern Tennessee.

After a rough flight, she crash-landed in an empty field in rural Connecticut. She decided this place would do as well as any other.

To get started in her new life, she closed her eyes and wished for a big house and a million dollars. Then she laid an egg.

The egg was small compared with all the other eggs she had been laying of late.

It cracked open. Inside was a 1937 cathedral radio.

"Odd!" clucked Starlight.

She laid another egg.
It cracked open to reveal a spinning wheel.
She laid a third and got an eggbeater.

"My chicken fairy godmother must be asleep
at the switch," Starlight said to herself.

As a matter of fact, Starlight's chicken fairy godmother was not asleep at the switch. She was not at the switch at all!

Now, being a chicken fairy godmother is hard work. And after years of service to many chickens, Melody D. Youngstown was worn out. She'd decided it was time to take a vacation cruise around the world.

Her replacement was her nephew Vernon, a harebrained hobbledehoy who got everyone's wishes mixed up, including Starlight's.

Eventually Starlight did lay a house, a lovely one-bedroom Colonial. She keeps herself busy laying new eggs, which provides her with plenty of bric-a-brac for a permanent yard sale. Starlight can never be sure what the next bungled-up wish will bring.